The Ocean Fairies

To Nadia Dale, a very special
friend of the fairies!

Special thanks
to Sue Mongredien

ORCHARD BOOKS
338 Euston Road, London NW1 3BH
Orchard Books Australia
Level 17/207 Kent Street, Sydney, NSW 2000
A Paperback Original

First published in 2010 by Orchard Books

A CIP catalogue record for this book is available
from the British Library.

ISBN 978 1 40830 817 2

1 3 5 7 9 10 8 6 4 2

Printed in Great Britain

The paper and board used in this paperback are natural recyclable
products made from wood grown in sustainable forests. The
manufacturing processes conform to the environmental regulations
of the country of origin.

Orchard Books is a division of Hachette Children's Books,
an Hachette UK company

www.hachette.co.uk

Pia
the Penguin Fairy

by Daisy Meadows

ORCHARD BOOKS

www.rainbowmagic.co.uk

The Magical Conch Shell at my side,
I'll rule the oceans far and wide!
But my foolish goblins have shattered the shell,
So now I cast my icy spell.

Seven shell fragments, be gone, I say,
To the human world to hide away,
Now the shell is gone, it's plain to see,
The oceans will never have harmony!

Contents

Ice to See You!

"Wheeee! This is fun!" squealed Kirsty
Tate, whizzing along on roller skates.
"Race you to that tree, Rachel!"

Kirsty's best friend, Rachel Walker,
grinned and sped along even faster on her
skateboard. "No worries," she called out
breathlessly, just overtaking Kirsty at the
last moment. "The winner!" she cheered,
slapping a hand to the trunk of the old
oak tree a split-second before Kirsty did.

The two girls laughed. It was a sunny spring day and they were on holiday together in the seaside resort of Leamouth, staying with Kirsty's gran for a whole week. Today they'd come out to Leamouth Park, which was at the top of Leamouth Cliffs, overlooking the sea.

"Doesn't the water look pretty with the sun shining on it?" Kirsty commented dreamily, staring out at the ocean below them.

It was a perfect blue, with thousands of twinkling lights dancing on the surface from the sun, and just a few ruffles of white where a breeze was whipping up the waves.

"I know," Rachel agreed. "It's so sparkly, it almost looks magical." Then she grinned at Kirsty. "Talking of magic, I hope we meet another Ocean Fairy today!"

"Me too," Kirsty said. "We're so lucky to be friends with the fairies, aren't we?"

"The luckiest girls in the world," Rachel agreed happily.

She and Kirsty had had lots of fairy adventures together so far, and at the start of this week, they'd fallen straight into another – this time with the Ocean Fairies. The girls were helping the Ocean Fairies look for the seven broken pieces of their Magical Golden Conch Shell, which kept the ocean world in order. Each piece of the shell was being guarded by the fairies' animal helpers, so the hunt was on to find them!

It had been horrid Jack Frost who had ordered his goblin servants to steal the Magical Conch Shell at the Fairyland Ocean Gala party. The clumsy goblins had ended up breaking the shell, though, which had caused all sorts of problems throughout the oceans. Now the broken pieces of shell were scattered across the

seas in the human world, and the girls and
their fairy friends were trying to find them
all before the goblins got their hands on
them again.

Kirsty and Rachel set off along the path
once more, and before very long, Kirsty
heard a tinkling tune drift over to them.
"Is that an ice-cream van?" she asked
hopefully, feeling
hungry at the
thought. Her
gran had
given them
some spending
money, and
it seemed a
long time since
breakfast all of
a sudden.

"Yes!" Rachel said, whizzing further down the path and spotting the colourful van parked up near the playground. It was still playing the jaunty tune while a large plastic ice cream rotated on the roof of the van. "Come on, let's go over and have a look."

The girls zoomed up to the van and gazed at the pictures of ice creams on the side. A friendly looking man with a white cap on his head leaned out of the hatch. "What can I get you, girls?" he asked.

"Orange crush, double choc pop, strawberry fizz… Ooh, how are we going to choose?" Kirsty said, licking her lips as she read. "What do you fancy, Rachel?" she asked. Then, when her friend didn't reply, she turned to her. "Rachel?"

Rachel didn't seem very interested in the list of ice creams, though. She was staring excitedly  up at the roof of the van where the plastic ice-cream cone was still turning.

And, as Kirsty looked up at it too,
she realised why. Perched on top of the
revolving plastic cone was a tiny smiling
fairy, waving down at them. It was Pia
the Penguin Fairy!

Pia had coffee-coloured skin and glossy
black hair which was
piled up on her
head and fastened
with a red bow.
She wore a
black and white
polka-dot dress
with a wide red
belt around the
middle, and
red pumps with
black bows on
her feet.

"What's it going to be, then?" the ice cream man asked. "Have you decided?"

"Um…no," Rachel said, unable to drag her eyes away from Pia as she fluttered off the plastic cone and hovered in mid air like a sparkly butterfly. The tiny fairy gestured to the girls to follow, then flew gracefully into a bush behind the ice-cream van. "Actually, I'm not that hungry after all," she said, smiling apologetically at the ice cream man. "Maybe later. Thanks anyway!"

She grabbed Kirsty's arm and they walked towards the bushes where they'd seen Pia flying.

"Over here!" they heard Pia's silvery voice call, and then Kirsty noticed a faint shimmer in the air, above one large flowering bush.

Feeling tingly with excitement, Kirsty and Rachel checked that nobody was looking, then sneaked behind the large bush, where they saw Pia sitting on a leaf and smiling at them. "Hello again," she said. "I'm so pleased to see you two.

I've got a feeling I know where Scamp, my little penguin, is, and I'm hoping he's guarding a piece of the Magical Golden Conch Shell. Will you help me look?"

Kirsty and Rachel didn't need to be asked twice. "Of course!" they said.

A dimple flashed in Pia's cheek as she smiled again. "I was hoping you would say that," she replied, and waved her wand through the air. "Let's go!"

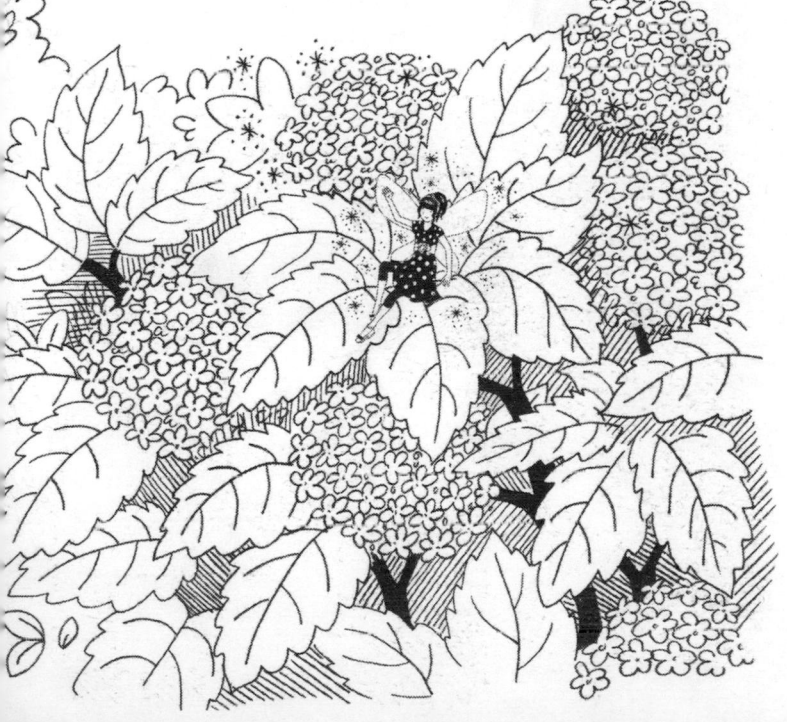

Let it
Snow

When Kirsty and Rachel had been at the
gala party in Fairyland, they had learned
that each of the Ocean Fairies had a
special magical animal helper, who lived
in the Royal Aquarium. After Jack Frost
had made the broken pieces of the conch
shell disappear, the Fairy Queen had
used her magic to send the magical
creatures out into the human world after
the shell pieces.

If the Ocean Fairies could find their animal again, they would know that a piece of the shell was nearby. So far, the girls had helped Ally the Dolphin Fairy and Amelie the Seal Fairy find their magical creatures as well as two pieces of the conch shell. But where would little Scamp the penguin be – and where was the third piece of the shell?

There was no time to think about that now though, because fairy magic was streaming from the end of Pia's wand and wrapping Kirsty, Rachel and Pia in a sparkly whirlwind that lifted them off the ground and spun them away at breath-taking speed.

"Whoaaa!" Kirsty squeaked. "This is even faster than my skates!"

After a few moments, the girls felt the whirlwind slow. Then their feet touched the ground once more, and they were able to look around.

"Wow," Rachel said, blinking in surprise. "Snow!"

"*Lots* of snow," Kirsty said in delight. It felt as if they'd landed in a winter wonderland, with soft white snow blanketing every surface.

They were standing at the edge of the shoreline, but it felt a million miles away from the beach at Leamouth, with its warm golden sand and twinkling blue sea. Here, the sea was full of floating ice floes and there was a freezing wind sweeping in from the water.

Luckily Pia's magic had changed the girls' clothes from the shorts and T-shirts they'd been wearing before, and they were now wrapped up snugly in thick snowsuits, hats, boots and gloves, feeling lovely and warm.

"Oh, look," Rachel gasped, pointing
ahead. "Polar bears! Aren't they
amazing?"

"Polar bears – ahh, we must
be at the North Pole,
then," Kirsty said,
feeling pleased
with herself for
remembering.

Pia shook her
head, looking
worried. "No
– this is the
South Pole," she
said. "Oh dear,
the polar bears
shouldn't be here! This
is all because the Golden
Conch Shell is missing.

Everything's topsy turvy in the oceans right now – it's even affected creatures who live *near* the oceans, like the polar bears."

"Well, there are some penguins at least," Rachel said, pointing to a group of the distinctive black and white birds who were huddled together on any icy patch near the water's edge.

"Can you see Scamp among them, Pia?"

Pia fluttered high into the air and scanned the crowd of birds. "Not from here," she replied. "Let's take a closer look."

The girls and Pia made their way across
the snow towards the penguins. As they
drew nearer, Kirsty noticed that some of
the taller penguins had something tucked
under their feathers above their feet, which
they occasionally fussed over with their
beaks. "What are they
doing?" she asked
Pia curiously.

Pia smiled.
"They're
the daddy
penguins,"
she replied,
"and they're
looking after
the eggs by
keeping them
warm on their feet.

It's a very important job."

Rachel watched one proud father penguin checking over his particular egg with his beak — but unfortunately he was rather *too* energetic about it. The next thing she knew, the egg had rolled right away from the penguin and was skidding over the slippery ice towards the sea.

"Oh no!" cried Rachel, breaking into a run. "We've got to catch that egg!"

Ready, Steady, Hatch!

The egg was heading right for the water and the girls hurried as fast as they could towards it. It was so difficult to run on the slippery snow, though! "If only we had our skates and skateboard," Kirsty cried helplessly, skidding on some ice and almost falling over.

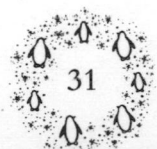

"Good thinking," Pia told her, waving
her wand. A flurry of blue sparkles
streamed from its tip all around the girls…
and in the very next second, a pair of ice
skates appeared on Kirsty's feet, and a
snowboard was under Rachel's.

"That's more like it," Rachel whooped,
whizzing over the snow and catching
the egg just before it
plopped into
the sea.

"Well done, Rachel," Kirsty said, skating up to join her. "And, look, here comes Daddy to collect it."

She and Rachel went to meet the daddy penguin who was waddling anxiously towards them. "Here you are," Rachel said, carefully setting the egg on the penguin's big black feet. "No damage done."

But then she heard a faint tapping sound…and looked down to see that the egg had cracked right across the middle. "Oh no!" she cried in alarm. "It *is* broken after all."

Pia, who'd flown over, landed lightly on the egg and inspected it. Then she looked up at the girls, her eyes sparkling. "Don't worry," she told them. "That crack is meant to be there. The chick inside is hatching out."

"Oh!" Kirsty cried excitedly. "What perfect timing! And now we get to see a newborn baby penguin – how brilliant!" Pia laughed at the delighted look on Kirsty's face.

"Not so fast," she warned. "It can take the babies a little while to break out of their eggs. This one might not hatch for some time."

But just as she was speaking, another, longer, crack appeared in the egg.

"Come on, little penguin," Rachel said encouragingly, crouching down. "You can do it!"

Tap, tap, tap, went the penguin chick from inside the egg.

"He's tapping away at it with his beak," Pia explained, as yet another crack appeared on the surface. This was the biggest crack so far. "Actually, I think we might just see him any second now…"

Crack! The eggshell broke clean in two and there sat a fluffy grey chick about the size of a tennis ball, with soft pink feet and tiny flippers.

"Oh my goodness," Kirsty breathed, unable to stop smiling. "That is just the cutest thing I've ever seen in my life!"

"Totally cute,"
Pia agreed,
as the daddy
penguin
bent down
to guide the
baby out
of the egg
for a cuddle.

"But now we really
should be... What's that noise?"

They turned at the sound of shouts,
and a roaring engine. A snowmobile was
approaching – and riding on it was a
group of people, all bundled up in bobble
hats and scarves. But they weren't just
ordinary people, Rachel realised, as she
noticed what long green noses they all
had...

"Oh no," she said. "The goblins are here! They must be looking for a piece of the conch shell, too."

"And they're really upsetting the penguins," Pia said anxiously, trying to calm a nearby daddy penguin who was looking very worried by the noise of the snowmobile.

The other penguins seemed
startled and jumpy by the
goblins' arrival too, and huddled
closer together to protect their
eggs. Meanwhile, some of the
other penguins walked away
from the goblins, flapping their
blunt flippers and making
snapping sounds with
their beaks.

"What are they doing?" Kirsty asked Pia, confused.

"It looks like they're trying to cause a diversion," she replied. "I think they're hoping to lead the goblins away from the new chick and the eggs." Then she gasped. "And there's Scamp – right at the front of the group. Maybe he knows

where the shell is!"

"Follow those penguins!" Rachel cried at once, setting off after them on her snowboard. "If Scamp has found the next piece of the conch shell then we've got to get to it before those goblins do. Come on!"

Trying Flying

The goblins had also noticed the group of penguins waddling away, and immediately turned their snowmobile around so that they could chase after them. "Hey, they're sneaking off!" the girls heard one of the goblins shout eagerly. "Maybe they know something about the missing conch shell. Come on, lads!"

"One of them is very sparkly, too. Look," a second goblin added, narrowing his eyes as he stared. He pointed at Scamp. "I bet he's got something to do with that shell! After them!"

Vrrrooom! went the snowmobile as it zoomed along, sending a shower of snow spraying up on each side as it went.

The penguins, meanwhile, were moving very strangely, flapping their wing-like flippers and taking little hops into the air before landing on their tummies and sliding along the snow.

Rachel stared as she followed them. "Are they trying to fly?" she asked Pia, baffled. "I didn't think penguins could."

Pia, who was perched on Kirsty's shoulder, looked just as surprised as Rachel. "They can't *usually* fly," she replied. "But they seem to think they can now! Everything's topsy-turvy because the Golden Conch Shell's been broken." She sighed. "If only the goblins hadn't smashed it before Shannon the Ocean Fairy could play the special tune on it, none of these strange things would be happening!"

"Still, the penguins are going pretty fast," Kirsty commented. "They're managing to keep ahead of the goblins at least."

But just then, the goblins roared forwards even faster on their snowmobile – and one of them leaned out daringly and made a grab for Scamp.

"Oh no!" Pia cried out anxiously. Then she gasped with relief. "Just missed him – thank goodness!"

"Knowing what goblins are like, they're sure to try again though," Rachel said. "We've got to stop them. Let me think…"

Kirsty giggled. "I've got an idea," she said suddenly, as she whizzed along on her skates. "Pia, do you think you'd be able to magic up a big snowman in front of the goblins? It would startle them, and hopefully make them slow down."

Rachel grinned. "Yes!" she said. "Maybe the snowman can be holding up a stop sign, like lollipop ladies do near schools? The goblins are so silly, they might even think it's a real person – like a lollipop snowman!"

Pia's dimples twinkled in her cheeks as she smiled. "That's a great idea," she agreed. "One lollipop snowman... coming up!"

She waved her wand, and a stream of pink sparkles whooshed out of it. A split-second later, a gigantic snowman, glittering with fairy magic, plopped down a short distance in front of the snowmobile. And yes, he was carrying a stop sign... only instead of saying 'Stop! Children Crossing' like a lollipop lady's sign, it said 'Stop! Penguins Crossing'!

"STOP!" yelled the goblins to the driver, all looking alarmed at the sight. "Whoa!" the goblin driving the snowmobile yelped, swerving to a halt. The penguins, meanwhile, carried on their funny flying-sliding-waddling and managed to get further away across the snow.

"Hang on a minute," one of the goblins said, peering at the snowman. "Why is it all sparkly like that?" He glanced around and then spotted Rachel and Kirsty whizzing up behind them. "Oh, right. Pesky girls and their fairy friend – *that's* why the snowman is sparkly. They just magicked it up here!"

The goblins stuck their tongues out

at the girls and drove around the snowman, before chasing after the penguins again. The penguins were now half-sliding and half-flying down a steep slope... Rachel blinked as they suddenly disappeared from view. "Where did they go?" she yelled in alarm, trying to slow down. But the slope was so steep, she found herself going faster and faster down it. "I can't stop!" she shouted in fright.

"Neither can I!" called Kirsty, who, in her panic, had completely forgotten how to slow down on ice skates. "And I think this is the edge of a cliff!"

The goblins were shouting too. "Use the brake! Use the brake!" the ones in the back yelled to the driver. "Stop!"

"Turn sideways!" Pia called to the girls. "Now!"

Rachel and Kirsty turned as hard as they could, and luckily both managed to stop just in time, right on the cliff edge. "Phew," Rachel breathed, panting and feeling shaky. "That was close."

The goblins, meanwhile, had managed to stop the snowmobile, but the driver had braked so sharply, they'd all been flung right out of it, and were now tumbling down the slope, gathering snow as they went.

"It's a goblin snowball," Kirsty said, her eyes wide at the sight of the huge white ball, with green arms and legs sticking out of it, all waving furiously. "And it's heading straight for us!"

"They're going to knock us over the cliff!" cried Rachel.

A Crystal Cavern

Quick as a flash, Pia waved her wand. Sparkling fairy dust billowed around the girls and then, just as the goblins were about to crash into them, Kirsty and Rachel felt themselves shrinking down smaller and smaller...and then gossamer wings sprouted on their backs. They were fairies again!

Down tumbled the goblins off the
cliff…and up fluttered the three fairies,
in the nick of time!

"Phew," gasped
Kirsty, her heart
thumping at the
close escape.
"Thank you,
Pia."

Pia was
busily waving
her wand
again, though.
"Much as those
goblins annoy me,
I'd better give them a
soft landing," she explained, and the girls
saw a huge drift of soft powdery snow
appear beneath the falling goblins.

Plop! Splat! Splurge!

The goblins dropped into the snowdrift and sank. Snow flew everywhere as they scrabbled to get out, their arms and legs waving wildly.

"Let's leave them to it and fly after the penguins," Rachel suggested. "I can't see them anywhere now, can you two?"

"No," Pia said, looking around. "Let's swoop down low. We might be able to pick up their trail."

The three friends soared
over the cliff, their hair
streaming back in
the wind as
they flew.

Once they were closer to the
ground, Kirsty spotted some distinctive
penguin footprints.

"They're heading this way!" she called,
pointing ahead. "Come on, let's follow
them."

At first sight, the footprints seemed to lead
straight into an icy wall, but as the fairies
flew nearer, they realised that the 'wall'
was actually the entrance of an icy cavern.

The big snow-covered archway that led to the cavern was almost invisible against the pure white landscape.

"Ugh, my feet are so cold and wet," Rachel heard the goblins grumbling. She turned quickly to see that they had all clambered out of the snowdrift and were looking very grumpy.

"Quick, let's fly inside the cavern," she said in a low voice, not wanting the goblins to notice them.

Pia and Kirsty agreed, and they all
darted into the gleaming cavern. Glittering
icicles hung from its roof, and the walls
and ground were covered in thousands of
twinkling ice crystals. "There's Scamp!"
Pia cried in delight, flying over to a cute
little penguin who was standing in the
middle of the cavern.

"Hello!" he squeaked
excitedly as he saw
her, and waddled
over to her at
once. "It's up
there," he said,
gesturing up
at the ceiling
with one
of his
flippers.

"So it is," Rachel exclaimed, gazing up and beaming as she saw the sparkles shining from the ceiling. "The shell piece has been frozen into one of the icicles!"

"Oh, clever Scamp," Pia said, kissing his cheek. "Well done for finding it. Now then…how are we going to get this down?"

She, Rachel and Kirsty flew up for a closer look at the shell-icicle. But before they could say another word, they heard stomping footsteps…and in came the goblins.

"Aha! Fairies!" one of them said, pointing triumphantly. "And what's that they've found up there?"

"Ooh! Ooh! It's a piece of that magic shell!" a second goblin cheered.

The goblins whooped in delight. "Let's snowball it down!" one of them suggested, scooping up a handful of snow and packing it into a tight round snowball.

Splat! Splat! Splat! The goblins all copied their friend, throwing snowball after snowball at the icicle.

Kirsty, Rachel and Pia had to dodge out of the way as the icy balls whizzed towards them. "Hey!" Pia yelled. "Be careful! You don't want to break it!"

But the words had only just left her mouth when… *Smash!* The icicle shattered and the shell piece went flying.

"Get it!" shouted the goblins.

"Get it!" cried the girls.

Pop-up
Penguin

Luckily, the piece of conch shell landed just near Scamp and he immediately tucked it under the fluffy feathers above his feet, just as Kirsty and Rachel had seen the daddy penguins protect their eggs. The goblins lunged towards Scamp but the other penguins, seeing what was happening, huddled around Scamp to protect him.

"Out of the way, you lot," one of the goblins grumbled, trying to push through the penguins and receiving a few sharp jabs from their beaks for his rudeness.

"Ow! Stop pecking me! Ow!" he cried, rubbing his arm. The other goblins were also being pecked by the penguins, who were determined to keep their friend Scamp safe. "Where *is* Scamp?" Kirsty whispered from where they were hovering above the black and white birds.

Before Pia could answer, Scamp's head popped up from the penguin huddle. "Catch me if you can!" he squawked cheekily.

"Grab him!" one of the goblins yelled crossly, still trying to push through the penguin crowd.

But moments later, Scamp popped up from a different part of the huddle and gave another playful squawk. "Can't catch me!" he teased.

Pia giggled. "He's really winding those goblins up, isn't he?" she said. "But maybe I should get him out of there now…"

Scamp popped up again and one of the goblins made a lunge for him. He was just about to grab hold of the little penguin when Pia quickly waved her wand, magicking Scamp and the shell to fairy-size, then flying in to snatch them up herself. The goblins grabbed wildly for Pia, but she managed to fly high enough so that she was out of their reach.

"Let's get away from here," Rachel said, and the three fairies zoomed out of the cavern, with Pia holding Scamp and the shell piece close to her.

"We did it!" Pia cheered, cuddling Scamp tightly. "Well done, girls. Another piece of shell is safe – that's wonderful news."

"Not so wonderful for the goblins," Kirsty said, seeing them trudge out of the cavern below, looking very gloomy, and bickering about who was going to tell Jack Frost the bad news.

"No," Rachel agreed. "But the penguins seem happy. And look, they've stopped doing that strange trying-to-fly thing now."

Pia smiled as the penguins trooped out and waddled along the ice back to the sea. Once in the water, they began swimming and diving as normal. "I think it must be because we've found another piece of the shell," she said. "Bit by bit, the ocean is returning to how it should be. Hurrah!"

She stroked Scamp's glossy feathers.
"And now we should get the shell
piece back to the Royal Aquarium in
Fairyland, where it will be safe. Thanks
for everything, girls!"

"Thank *you*," Kirsty said, hugging her.
"That was fun!"

"Bye, Pia, bye, Scamp," Rachel said. "I
loved seeing all the penguins – especially
that little baby. So cute!"

Pia waved her wand and a flood of
fairy dust streamed around Kirsty and
Rachel, and instantly, they were
spun into the air very fast
in a glittery magic
whirlwind. Moments
later, they found
themselves back
in Leamouth
Park, and
they were
girls once
more, and
back in their
summery
clothes
with their
roller skates and
skateboard.

One thing was different though – they were each holding a huge cone, filled with pink and white scoops of ice cream and covered in edible sparkles!

"Yum!" Kirsty said in delight, taking a big lick of hers. "Delicious!" Rachel grinned and licked hers too. "Tastes magic to me," she said. "What an *ice* way to finish an adventure!"

The Ocean Fairies

Pia the Penguin Fairy has found
her piece of the Golden Conch
Shell! Now Rachel and Kirsty
must help...

Tess the Sea Turtle Fairy

A Magical Sandcastle

"Shall we build another tower, Kirsty?"
Rachel Walker asked her best friend,
Kirsty Tate.

The two girls were kneeling on the
beach, making an enormous sandcastle.
They'd been working on it all day in
the sunshine. The castle had turrets and
archways, as well as a large moat all
around it.

"Oh, yes, brilliant idea!" Kirsty said with
a grin. She picked up her bucket. "Let's
start decorating the castle, too. We can
use those pretty pink and white shells we
found earlier."

Carefully, Rachel began to build the tower. Meanwhile, Kirsty tipped the shells out of her bucket and began sorting through them.

"Look, Kirsty, the sun's starting to set," Rachel pointed out, noticing that people were packing up and leaving the beach. "We'll have to go back to your gran's soon." The girls were spending the spring school holiday in Leamouth with Kirsty's gran.

Kirsty's face fell. "I know we've had a lovely time on the beach, Rachel," she sighed, "but we haven't seen a *single* magical fairy sparkle all day! I was hoping we were going to find another missing piece of the Magical Golden Conch Shell."

"Me, too," Rachel agreed. "But don't

forget what Queen Titania always says –
we *have* to wait for the magic to come to
us!"

On the first day of their holiday, the girls
had been thrilled to receive an invitation
to the Fairyland Ocean Gala. There
they'd met their old friend, Shannon the
Ocean Fairy, as well as the other Ocean
Fairies and their Magical Creatures.
The highlight of the gala was to be
the moment when Shannon played the
beautiful Golden Conch Shell. This would
make sure that there was peace, harmony
and order in all the oceans of the world
for the next year.

But before Shannon had a chance to
play her magical tune, Jack Frost and his
goblins had burst onto the scene. On Jack
Frost's orders, the goblins had grabbed the

Golden Conch Shell, but as they argued over it, the Conch Shell had fallen to the ground and smashed into seven shining pieces.

Jack Frost had immediately raised his ice wand and, with a burst of freezing magic, he'd scattered the seven fragments in different hiding places throughout the human world. Shannon, Rachel, Kirsty, and all the fairies had been horrified.

They knew that without the Golden Conch Shell, there would be chaos and confusion in the oceans...

The Ocean Fairies

Win Rainbow Magic goodies!

In every book in the Ocean Fairies series
(books 85-91) there is a hidden picture of a shell with a
letter in it. Find all seven letters and re-arrange them to
make a special Ocean Fairies word, then send it to us.
Each month we will put the entries into a draw and select
one winner to receive a Rainbow Magic sparkly T-shirt
and goody bag!

Send your entry on a postcard to Rainbow Magic Ocean
Fairies Competition, Orchard Books, 338 Euston Road,
London NW1 3BH. Australian readers should write to
Hachette Children's Books, Level 17/207 Kent Street,
Sydney, NSW 2000.
New Zealand readers should write to Rainbow Magic
Competition, 4 Whetu Place, Mairangi Bay, Auckland,
NZ. Don't forget to include your name and address.
Only one entry per child.
Final draw: 30th April 2011.

Have you checked out the

website at:
www.rainbowmagic.co.uk

Meet the Twilight Fairies
in September 2010!

Ava the Sunset Fairy
978-1-40830-906-3

Lexi the Firefly Fairy
978-1-40830-907-0

Zara the Starlight Fairy
978-1-40830-908-7

Morgan the Midnight Fairy
978-1-40830-909-4

Yasmin the Night Owl Fairy
978-1-40830-910-0

Maisie the Moonbeam Fairy
978-1-40830-911-7

Sabrina the Sweet Dreams Fairy
978-1-40830-912-4